Dear Parents:

Congratulations! Your child is taking the first steps on an exciting journey. The destination? Independent reading!

STEP INTO READING® will help your child get there. The program offers five steps to reading success. Each step includes fun stories and colorful art or photographs. In addition to original fiction and books with favorite characters, there are Step into Reading Non-Fiction Readers, Phonics Readers and Boxed Sets, Sticker Readers, and Comic Readers—a complete literacy program with something to interest every child.

Learning to Read, Step by Step!

Ready to Read   Preschool–Kindergarten
• big type and easy words • rhyme and rhythm • picture clues
For children who know the alphabet and are eager to begin reading.

Reading with Help   Preschool–Grade 1
• basic vocabulary • short sentences • simple stories
For children who recognize familiar words and sound out new words with help.

Reading on Your Own   Grades 1–3
• engaging characters • easy-to-follow plots • popular topics
For children who are ready to read on their own.

Reading Paragraphs   Grades 2–3
• challenging vocabulary • short paragraphs • exciting stories
For newly independent readers who read simple sentences with confidence.

Ready for Chapters   Grades 2–4
• chapters • longer paragraphs • full-color art
For children who want to take the plunge into chapter books but still like colorful pictures.

STEP INTO READING® is designed to give every child a successful reading experience. The grade levels are only guides; children will progress through the steps at their own speed, developing confidence in their reading.

Remember, a lifetime love of reading starts with a single step!

Visit us on the Web!
StepIntoReading.com
randomhousekids.com

Educators and librarians, for a variety of teaching tools, visit us at RHTeachersLibrarians.com

ISBN 978-1-5247-6413-5 (trade) — ISBN 978-1-5247-6414-2 (lib. bdg.)

Printed in the United States of America

10 9 8 7 6

STEP INTO READING®

nickelodeon

PAW PATROL

MISSION·PAW

based on the teleplay "Mission Paw"
by Steve Sullivan and Andy Guerdat

illustrated by Nate Lovett

Random House 🏠 New York

Chase is on the case
in an all-new place!
His mission
is in Barkingburg.

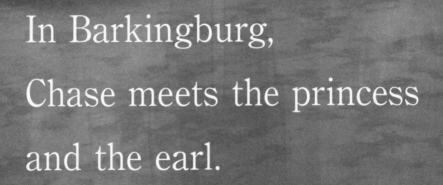

In Barkingburg,
Chase meets the princess
and the earl.

He also meets
the royal dog.
Her name is Sweetie.

Chase guards
the Barkingburg crown.

Sweetie puts on the crown.
She wants to be queen!

Chase sees Sweetie
wearing the crown.
His bow tie is
a camera.
He makes a video.

Sweetie stops Chase!
He is locked
in the dungeon!
He calls
for help.

12

PAW Patrol

to the rescue!

Zuma searches
the castle's moat.

<u>Knock, knock, knock!</u>

Zuma hears something.

Is Chase knocking on

the wall?

Rubble's Mini Miner
can help!

Rubble drills through
the castle wall.

Chase is safe!

Chase shows his video
to the earl and the princess.
They learn that Sweetie
took the crown.

Sweetie tries to escape.

Skye stops her.

The crown is safe again!

Chase, Skye,
Marshall, Rubble,
and Zuma

are all good pups!